Romantasy Embroidery

23 Stunning Patterns for Romance and Fantasy Lovers

JAMIE PHOTO

DOVER PUBLICATIONS
Garden City, New York

Copyright © 2026 by Jamie Photo
All rights reserved. No part of this publication may be reproduced, downloaded, distributed, transmitted, or stored in any form or by any means, electronic or mechanical, without prior written permission from the publisher.

Romantasy Embroidery: 23 Stunning Patterns for Romance and Fantasy Lovers is a new work, first published by Dover Publications in 2026.

ISBN-13: 978-0-486-85491-5
ISBN-10: 0-486-85491-4

Publisher: Betina Cochran
Acquisitions Editor: Allyson D'Antonio
Managing Editorial Supervisor: Susan Rattiner
Production Editor: Gregory Koutrouby
Cover Designer: Jamie Photo
Creative Manager and Interior Designer: Marie Zaczkiewicz
Production: Pam Weston, Tammi McKenna, Ayse Yilmaz

Printed in China
85491401   2025
www.doverpublications.com

Table of Contents

Introduction 4
Pattern Transfer Instructions 5
Stitches Used in This Book 6
Stitch Guide Swatches 10

Teacup
12

Cauldron
16

Mountain Flower
20

Dragon Book
24

Darling
28

Heart Book
32

Painting
36

Through Love
40

Mushroom
44

Dragon Moon
48

Lily of the Valley
52

Mage Hand
56

Lupine
60

Morally Grey
64

I'd Rather Be Reading
68

Angel Wings
72

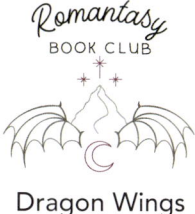
Dragon Wings
76

Mask
80

Skull and Books
84

Sword and Wings
88

Dragon Sword
92

Considerable Length
96

Pine Cone
100

Templates
105

Introduction

Hi there, and welcome!

I'm Jamie, the artist and embroidery designer behind *Jamie Photo*. I'm so excited to share this magical collection of embroidery patterns with you!

As a lifelong embroidery lover and full-time creative, I've built my small business around designing hand-drawn patterns inspired by the things I adore most: whimsical nature, dreamy romance, and all things geeky and fantastical. *Romantasy Embroidery* is a true passion project—a celebration of magic, fierce heroines, enchanted creatures, and tender moments stitched into fabric.

Inside this book, you'll find **23 stunning embroidery patterns** inspired by romantic fantasy themes. From celestial motifs and spells to sword-wielding designs and cozy cottagecore vibes, there's something here to enchant every fantasy and romance lover. Each design includes stitch guides to help bring your hoop to life—whether you're a seasoned stitcher or brand new to embroidery.

If you're looking for even more patterns, tutorials, or just some cozy crafting inspiration, you can find me online at www.ShopJamiePhoto.com and on YouTube, where I share embroidery tips, technique breakdowns, and behind-the-scenes peeks into my creative process.

Thank you so much for picking up this book. I hope it inspires you to slow down, get cozy, and create something truly magical—one stitch at a time.

Happy stitching,

Jamie
Artist & Embroidery Designer

Pattern Transfer Instructions

There are multiple ways to transfer your pattern onto your fabric. Here are a few of my favorites. The first two options work best for white or thin fabrics. The third option is great for black fabric or clothing.

Option One: Tracing from Book

- You can trace the pattern straight from the book if you're happy with the sizing.
- Lay your embroidery hoop with fabric flat or "backward" over the book page. This will allow you to draw directly onto the fabric with either a pencil or a washable fabric pen.

Option Two: Scanning + Tracing

- Scan your pattern with either a printer or photo. This will also allow you to resize your design.
- Print out your design, and tape to a sunny window or use a light box. This lets light through the back of your paper, to better show through the fabric.
- Lay your embroidery hoop with fabric flat or "backward" over the printout. This will allow you to draw directly onto the fabric with either a pencil or a washable fabric pen.

Option Three: Scanning + Water-Soluble Fabric

- Scan your pattern with either a printer or photo. This will also allow you to resize your design.
- Print out your design onto a water-soluble stick and stitch paper that you can peel and stick right onto your fabric. My favorite brand is called Sulky.
- Stitch over top and wash away the paper with warm water once you're done.

Stitches Used in This Book

Back Stitch

 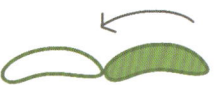 

1. Bring your needle up through the fabric where you'd like your chain of back stitches to begin. Place your needle the desired distance away from the start of your first stitch. Go down through the fabric to complete the first stitch.

2. Space your stitches an even length apart, bringing the needle up through the fabric at that distance. Complete your next stitch by bringing your needle back down through the end of the previous stitch.

3. Continue this process along your chain of back stitches—a great beginner stitch for lettering, outlines, and more.

Fill/Brick Stitch

1. Start by outlining your design with a chain of split stitches.

2. Then, create a chain of split stitches going down the middle of your design.

3. Space the following chains of split stitches to mark the correct angle of the following stitches you would like to create.

4. Fill in the remaining space with a combination of back stitches and split stitches.

5. Continue this process to fill in large areas of a design where you desire more texture in your stitches.

French Knot Stitch

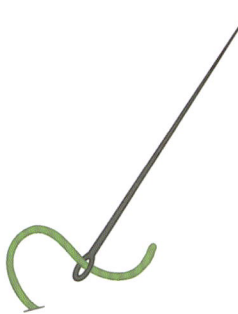 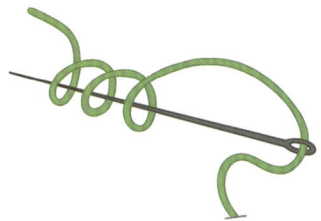  

1. Bring your needle up through the fabric where you would like your French knot to be placed.

2. Wrap your thread around the tip of the needle three times. Make sure to keep your needle close to the fabric.

3. Angle your needle back down through the fabric very close to your first hole. Keep the thread tightly wrapped around the needle until you have pulled all the thread through.

4. Continue this process to create the center of a flower by placing your knots very close to one another, or to create starts scattered around your designs.

Lazy Daisy Stitch

1. Bring your needle up through the fabric where you want the base of your petal to be.

2. Take your needle back down through that same hole, leaving a little loop of thread remaining.

3. Bring your needle back up through the fabric where you want to anchor down your petal, and make sure to come up through the inside of the petal.

4. Create a small stitch around your petal to secure the petal in place. Make sure not to pull any of these stitches too tightly, to leave your petals looking plump.

5. Repeat the process to create each petal of a flower or individual leaves along a stem.

Stitch Guide 7

Long Stitch

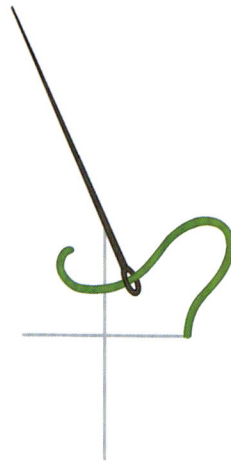

1. Bring your needle up through the fabric where you would like your long stitch to begin.

2. Follow the angle and distance of your pattern to create one single long stitch over the fabric. Bring your needle back down where you would like this stitch to end.

3. Repeat the process to create shapes such as stems, angular outlines, or stars by crisscrossing your stitches.

Satin Stitch

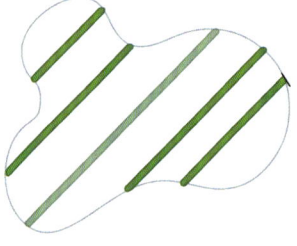

1. Bring your needle up through your fabric along the outer edge of your design area. Hold your thread over the fabric to mark the angle of your first stitch. Bring your thread back down through the opposite edge of your design area.

2. Space out your satin stitches along the design area to mark the desired angle or length of the stitches to follow.

3. Then, fill in the remaining space of your design area with smooth, evenly spaced stitches to make everything seamless.

4. One of the most versatile stitches that can be used to create leaves, fill in flower petals, and more, the satin stitch can be created at any angle you desire.

Split Stitch

1. Bring your needle up through the fabric where you'd like your chain of split stitches to begin. Place your needle the desired distance away and go down through the fabric to complete your first stitch.

2. Bring your needle back up through the fabric about a half-stitch distance away.

3. Bring your thread back over your previous stitch and go down through the middle of that stitch, making sure to split the stitch evenly.

4. Continue this process to make a chain of split stitches. This should end up looking slightly like a braid from the top.

5. This is the most forgiving beginner stitch. It is great for making seamless straight lines, lettering, and any outline with curves.

Stem Stitch

1. Bring your needle up through your fabric where you would like your chain of stem stitches to begin. Set your desired stitch length by going back down through the fabric, but leave a small loop of thread above your fabric.

2. Hold this loop over to the side, and come back up through your fabric about halfway between this stitch.

3. Pull the thread tight to make the loop lay flat.

4. Continue this process of leaving loose thread with your next stitch, then coming back up halfway before pulling it tight.

5. This stitch works well for anything with curves. Use it to make perfect circles, moons, or stems.

Stitch Guide 9

Teacup

Color Guide

Blue #931

Tan #840

Gold #G3821

Grey #453

Black #310

Teacup 13

Stitch Guide

Steps

1.
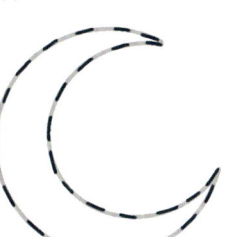

2.
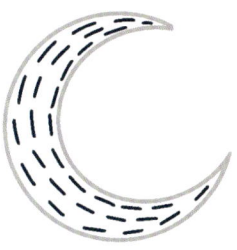

1. Back Stitch, #G3821
2. Back Stitch Fill, #G3821
3. Split Stitch, #310, 2-ply
4. Split Stich, #840, 2-ply
5. Back Stitch, #G3821
6. Back Stitch, #453, 2-ply
7. Split Stitch, #310, 2-ply

3.

4.

5.
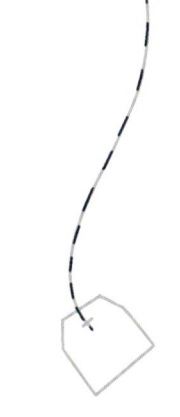

6.

7.
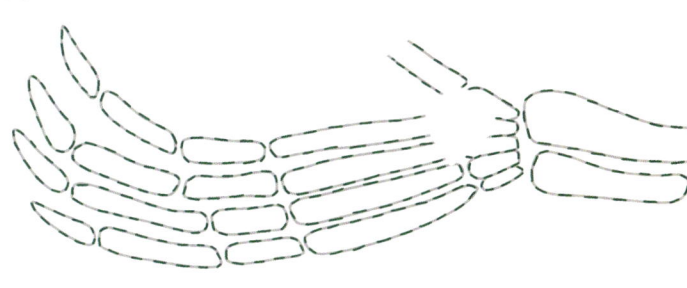

Teacup 15

Cauldron

Color Guide

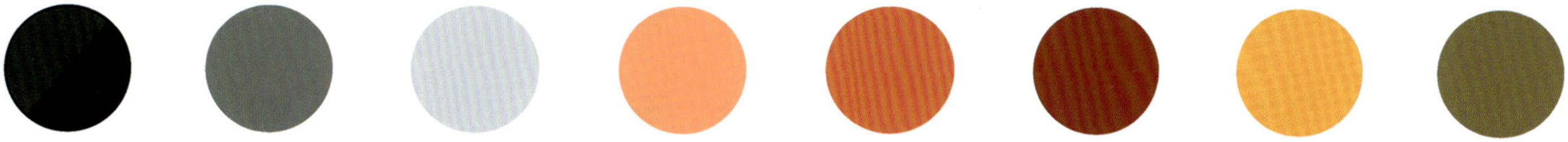

Black
#310

Light Grey
#414

White
#BLANC

Light Salmon Pink
#3778

Darker Salmon
#3830

Brick
#300

Yellow
#435

Green
#3011

Cauldron

Stitch Guide

Steps

1.

2.

3.

1. Split Stitch, 3-ply, #3011
2. Satin Stitch, 2-ply, #3011
3. Satin Stitch, 2-ply, #300
4. Satin Stitch, 2-ply, #435
5. French Knot, 3-ply, #435
6. Satin Stitch, 2-ply, #3778
7. Satin Stitch, 2-ply, #3830
8. Satin Stitch, 2-ply, #3830
9. French Knot, 3-ply, #435
10. Split Stitch, 2-ply, #310
11. Fill Stitch, 2-ply, #310
12. Satin Stitch, 2-ply, #414
13. Split Stitch, 3-ply, #BLANC

4.

5.

6.

7.

8.

9.

10.

11.

12.

13.

Cauldron 19

Mountain Flower

Color Guide

Brick #975   Navy Blue #3799   Light Blue #926   Black #310

Mountain Flower 21

Stitch Guide

Steps

1.
2.
3.

1. Split Stitch, 3-ply, #3799
2. Satin Stitch, 3-ply, #3799
3. Satin Stitch, 3-ply, #926
4. Satin Stitch, 3-ply, #3799
5. French Knot, 3-ply, #3799
6. Satin Stitch, 3-ply, # 975
7. Lazy Daisy, 3-ply, #975
8. French Knot, 3-ply, #3799
9. French Knot, 3-ply, # 926
10. Split Stitch, 3-ply, #310
11. Long Stitch, 2-ply, #310
12. Long Stitch, 3-ply, #3799
13. French Knot, 3-ply, #975

4.
5.
6.

7.
8.
9.

10.
11.
12.
13.

Mountain Flower

Dragon Book

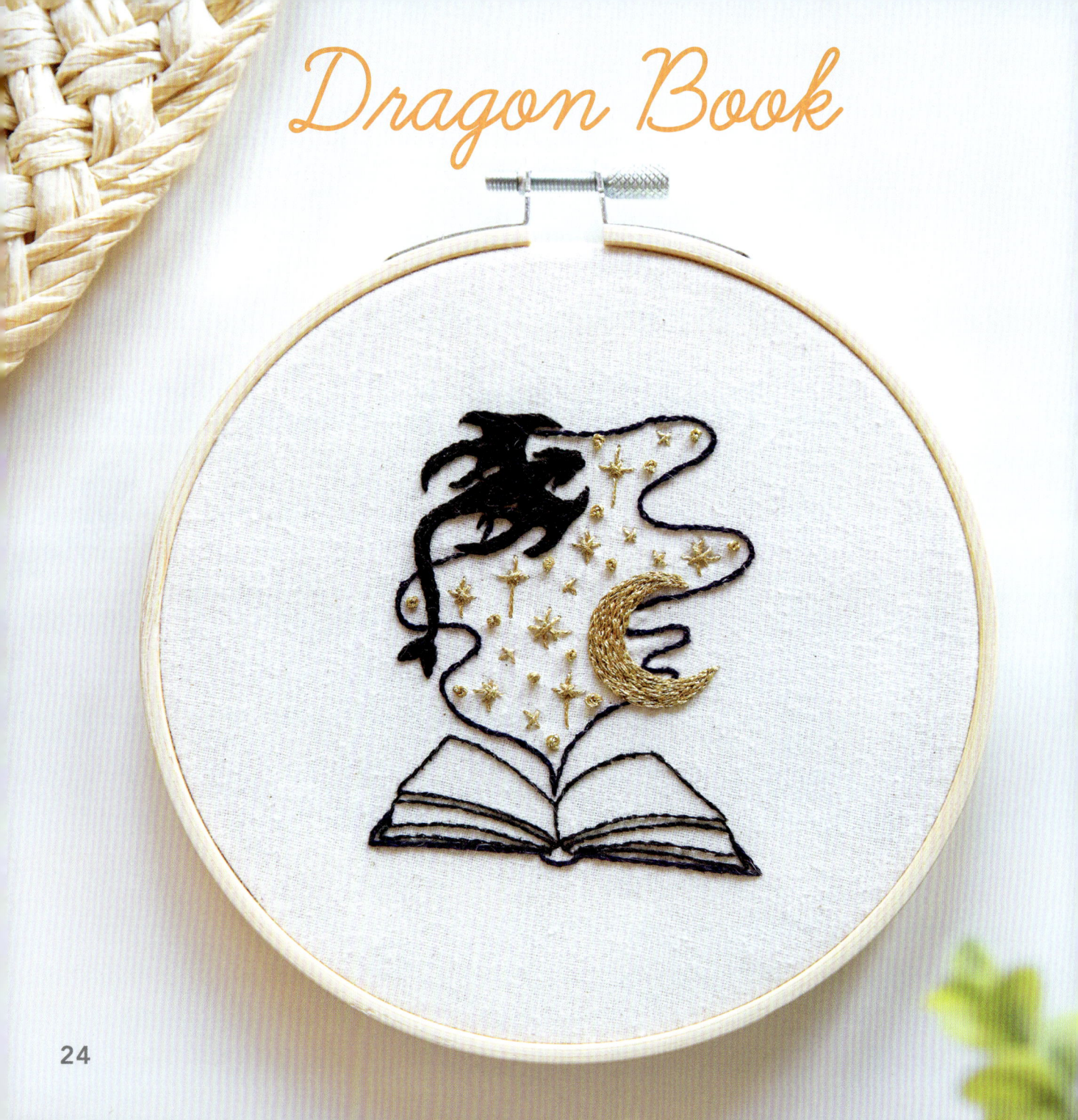

Color Guide

Black
#310

Gold
#G3821

Blue
#939

Stitch Guide

Steps

1.

2.

3.

1. Split Stitch, 1-ply, #310
2. Fill Stitch, 2-ply, #310
3. Split Stitch, #G3821
4. Fill Stitch, #G3821
5. Split Stitch, 2-ply, #939
6. French Knot, #G3821
7. Long Stitch, #G3821
8. Split Stitch, 2-ply, #310
9. Split Stitch, 2-ply, #939

4.

5.

6.

7.

8.

9.

Dragon Book 27

Darling

Color Guide

| Dark Purple #154 | Medium Purple #3835 | Light Purple #153 | Black #310 |

Stitch Guide

Steps

1.

2.

1. Split Stitch, 2-ply, #310
2. Split Stitch, 2-ply, #154 + #3835 + #153
3. Long Stitch, 2-ply, #154
4. Long Stitch, 2-ply, #3835
5. Long Stitch, 2-ply, #153
6. French Knot, 2-ply, #154 + #3835 + #153

3.

4.

5.

6.

Heart Book

Color Guide

		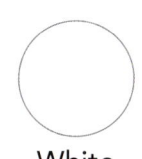						
Black #310	Grey #648	White #BLANC	Yellow #436	Light Teal #3817	Dark Teal #3808	Light Pink #352	Dark Pink #3830	Green #3012

Heart Book

Stitch Guide

Steps

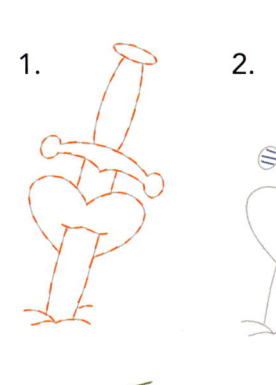
1.

2.

3.

4.

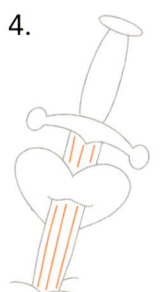

5.

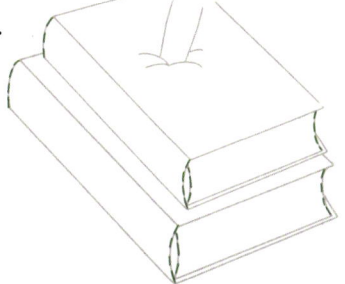
6.

1. Split Stitch, 1-ply, #310
2. Satin Stitch, 2-ply, #436
3. Satin Stitch, 2-ply, #3830
4. Satin Stitch, 2-ply #648
5. Long Stitch, 2-ply, #310
6. Split Stitch, 2-ply, #310
7. Satin Stitch, 2-ply, #3817 + #3808
8. Satin Stitch, 2-ply, #BLANC
9. Satin Stitch, 2-ply #3830
10. Satin Stitch, 2-ply, #352
11. Satin Stitch, 2-ply, #3012
12. Satin Stitch, 2-ply, #352
13. French Knot, 3-ply, #436

7.

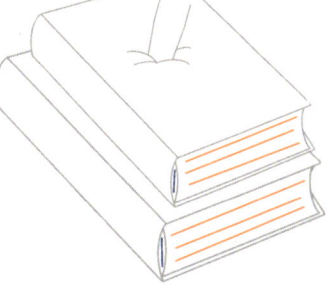
8.

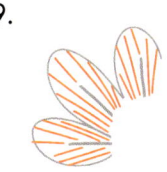
9.

10.

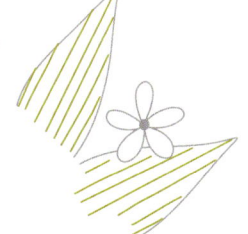
11.

12.

13.

Heart Book

Painting

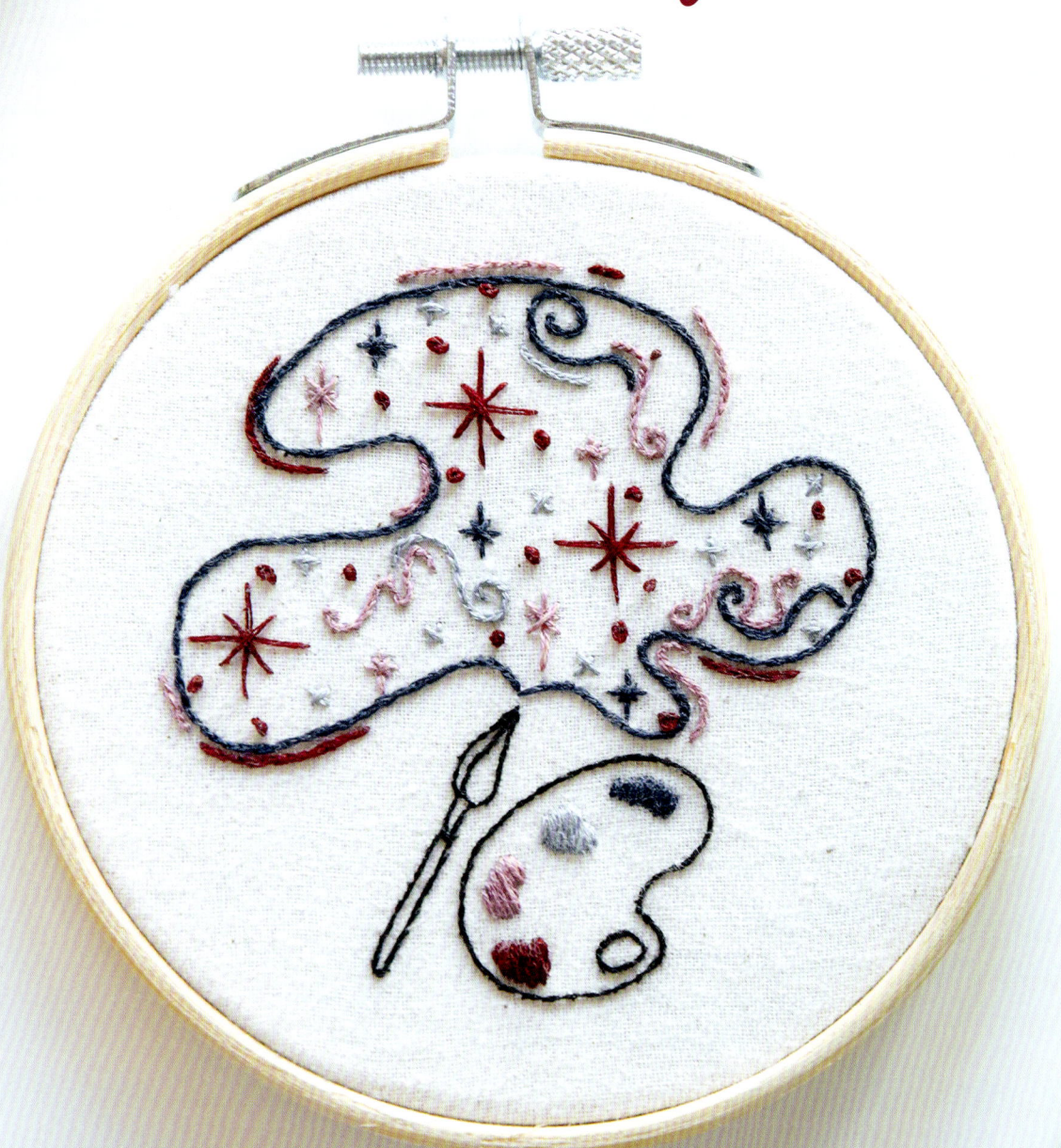

Color Guide

Black
#310

Dark Purple
#814

Light Purple
#316

Light Blue
#932

Dark Blue
3750

Stitch Guide

Steps

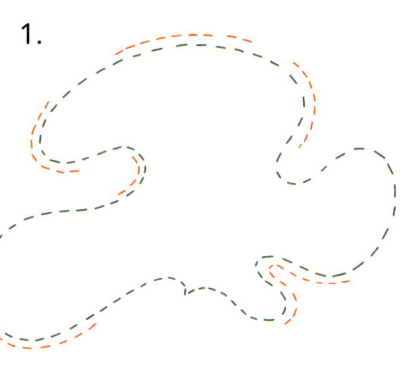
1.

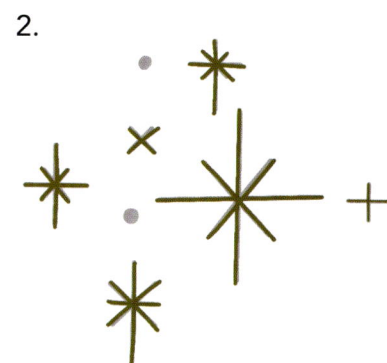
2.

1. Split Stitch, 2-ply, #3750 + #814 + #316
2. Long Stitch, 2-ply, #3750 + #932 + #316 + #814
3. French Knot, 2-ply, #814
4. Split Stitch, 2-ply, #3750 + #932 + #316
5. Split Stitch, 2-ply, #310
6. Satin Stitch, 2-ply, #3750 + #932 + #316 + #814

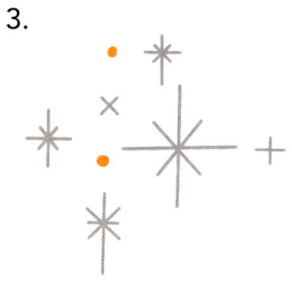
3.

4.

5.

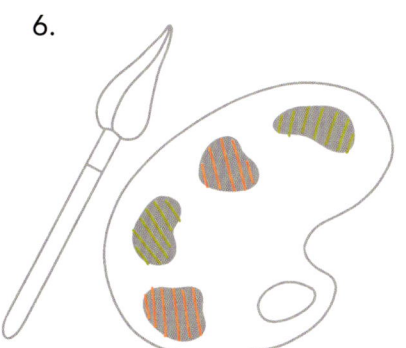
6.

Painting

Through Love

Color Guide

Gold
#G3821

Stitch Guide

Steps

1. Split Stitch, #G3821
2. Back Stitch, #G3821
3. Split Stitch, #G3821
4. Back Stitch, #G3821
5. Split Stitch, #G3821
6. Long Stitch, #G3821
7. Long Stitch, #G3821
8. French Knot Stitch, #G3821

Mushroom

44

Color Guide

Maroon
#3777

Beige
#945

Yellow
#436

Green
#935

White
#BLANC

Mushroom 45

Stitch Guide

Steps

1.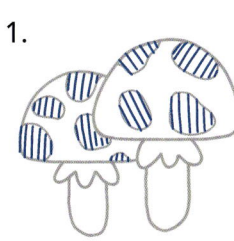
2.
3.
4.
5.
6.
7.
8.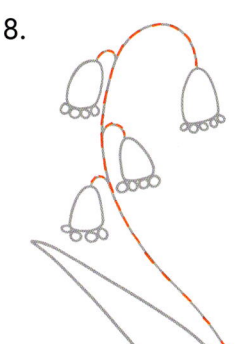
9.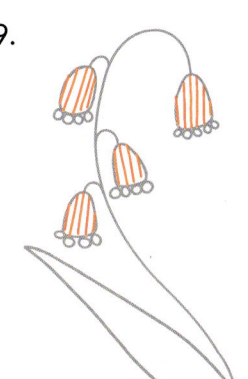
10.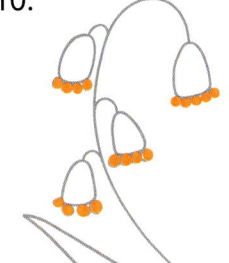
11.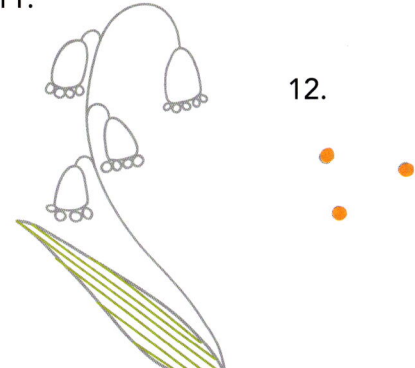

1. Satin Stitch, 2-ply, #BLANC
2. Satin Stitch, 2-ply, #3777
3. Satin Stitch, 2-ply, #945
4. Satin Stitch, 2-ply, #945
5. Split Stitch, 2-ply, #436
6. Long Stitch, 2-ply, #436
7. Satin Stitch, 2-ply, #436
8. Split Stitch, 2-ply, #935
9. Satin Stitch, 2-ply, #BLANC
10. French Knot Stitch, 2-ply, #BLANC
11. Satin Stitch, 2-ply, #935
12. French Knot Stitch, 2-ply, #436

Mushroom 47

Dragon Moon

Color Guide

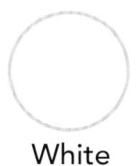

White
#BLANC

Black
#310

Dragon Moon

Stitch Guide

Steps

1. Split Stitch, 1-ply, #BLANC
2. Fill Stitch, 1-ply, #BLANC
3. Split Stitch, 2-ply, #BLANC
4. Satin Stitch, 1-ply, #BLANC
5. Satin Stitch, 2-ply, #BLANC
6. Back Stitch, 2-ply, #BLANC
7. Split Stitch, 2-ply, #310
8. Split Stitch/Fill Stitch, 1-ply, #310
9. Split Stitch, 1-ply, #310
10. Fill Stitch, 2-ply, #310
11. French Knot Stitch, 2-ply, #BLANC
12. French Knot Stitch, 2-ply, #BLANC

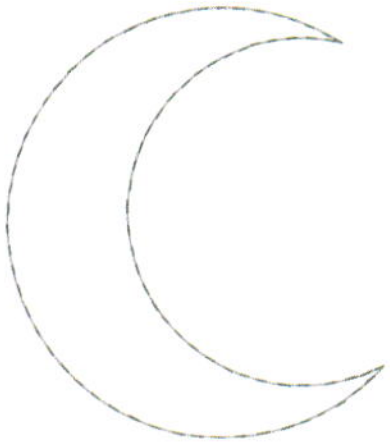

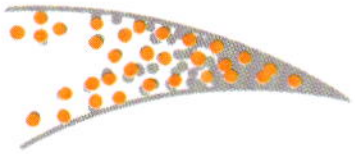

Dragon Moon 51

Lily of the Valley

Color Guide

White
#BLANC

Gold
#E436

Green
#935

Lily of the Valley 53

Stitch Guide

Steps

1.

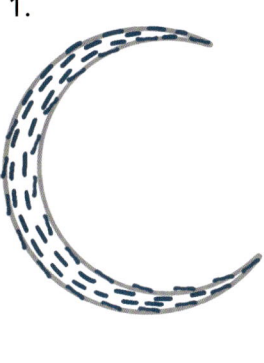

2.

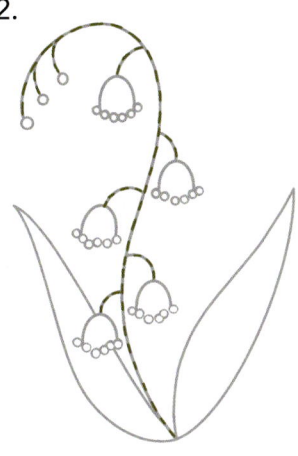

3.

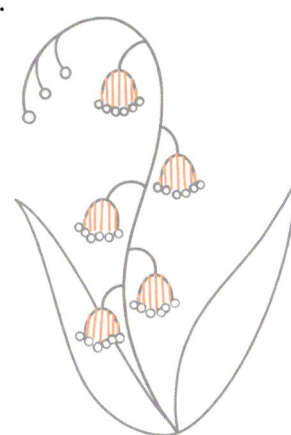

1. Stem Stitch, #E436
2. Split Stitch, 3-ply, #935
3. Satin Stitch, 3-ply, #BLANC
4. French Knot Stitch, 3-ply, #BLANC
5. Satin Stitch, 3-ply, #935
6. Long Stitch, #E436
7. French Knot Stitch, #E436

4.

5.

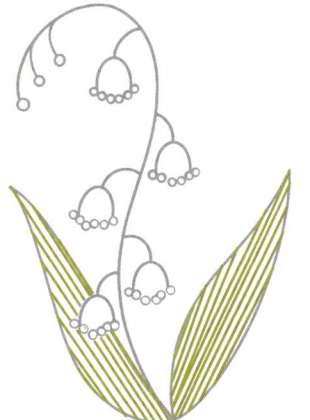

6.

7.

Lily of the Valley

Mage Hand

Color Guide

Black
#310

Red
#3721

Orange
#976

Yellow
#729

Stitch Guide

Steps

1.
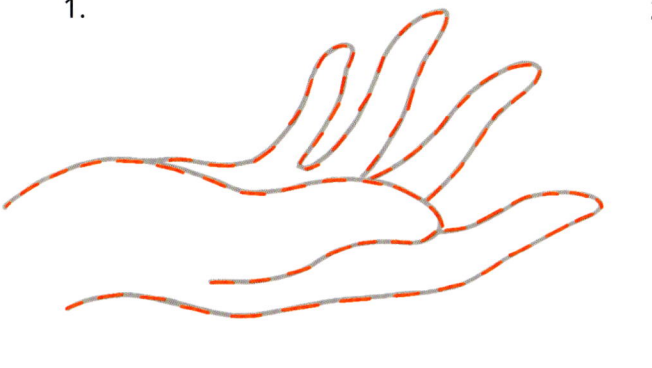

2.

1. Split Stitch, 3-ply, #310
2. Split Stitch, 2-ply, #3721 + #976 + #729
3. Split Stitch, 2-ply, #3721 + #976 + #729
4. Back Stitch, 2-ply, #729
5. French Knot, 2-ply, #729

3.
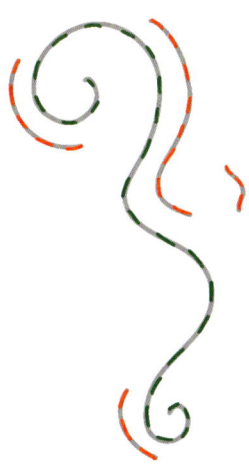

4.
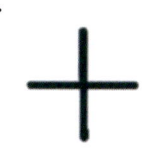

5.

Mage Hand

Lupine

Color Guide

Black
#310

Purple
#154

Green
#3051

Lupine

Stitch Guide

Steps

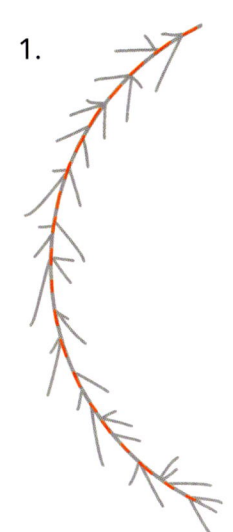

1.

2.

3.

4.

2-ply:
1. Split Stitch, #3051
2. Long Stitch, #3051
3. Satin Stitch, #310
4. French Knot Stitch, #310
5. Split Stitch, #3051
6. Satin Stitch, #154
7. Split Stitch, #310

5.

6.

7.

Lupine 63

Morally Grey

Color Guide

Morally Grey
BOOK CLUB

Black #310	Dark Grey #3799	Light Grey #414

Morally Grey 65

Stitch Guide

Steps

1.

2.

1. Split Stitch, 2-ply, #310
2. Split Stitch, 2-ply, #310
3. Split Stitch, 1-ply, #414
4. Back Stitch, 1-ply, #414
5. Back Stitch, 2-ply, #3799
6. French Knot Stitch, 2-ply, #3799
7. Split Stitch, 2-ply, #3799
8. Fill Stitch, 1-ply, #3799

3.

4.

5.

6.

7.

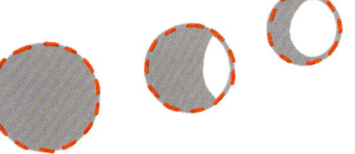

8.

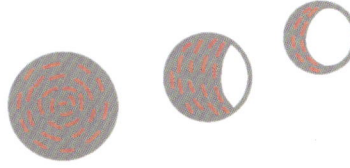

Morally Grey

I'd Rather Be Reading

Color Guide

I'D RATHER BE READING

Black
#310

Purple
#814

Dark Green
#934

Light Green
#3011

Stitch Guide

Steps

1.
2.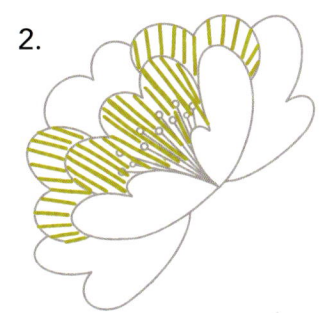

1. Long Stitch, 1-ply, #310
2. Satin Stitch, 3-ply, #814
3. Satin Stitch, 3-ply, #814
4. French Knot, 3-ply, #310
5. Split Stitch, 3-ply, #934
6. Satin Stitch, 3-ply, #934
7. Split Stitch, 3-ply, #3011
8. Satin Stitch, 3-ply, #3011
9. Split Stitch, 2-ply, #310

3.
4.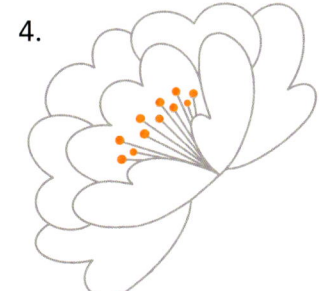

5.
6.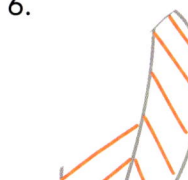
7.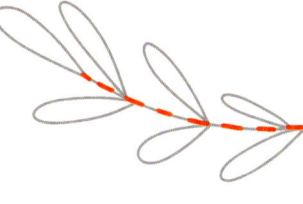

8.
9. RATHER

I'd Rather Be Reading   71

Angel Wings

Color Guide

romantasy
BOOK CLUB

● Black #310   ● Gold #436

Stitch Guide

romantasy

BOOK CLUB

74   Angel Wings

Steps

1. Split Stitch, 2-ply, #310
2. Long Stitch, 3-ply, #436
3. Split Stitch, 2-ply, #310
4. Split Stitch, 3-ply, #436

1. romantasy BOOK CLUB

2.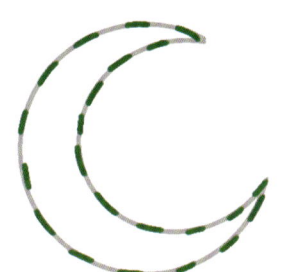

3.

4.

Angel Wings 75

Dragon Wings

Color Guide

Romantasy
BOOK CLUB

Black
#310

Purple
#154

Dark Grey
#3799

Light Grey
#414

Dragon Wings 77

Stitch Guide

Romantasy
BOOK CLUB

Steps

1.

1. Split Stitch, 2-ply, #310
2. Split Stitch, 3-ply, #3799
3. Split Stitch, 2-ply, #3799
4. Split Stitch, 3-ply, #414
5. Split Stitch, 3-ply, #154
6. Long Stitch, 3-ply, #154

2.

3.

4.

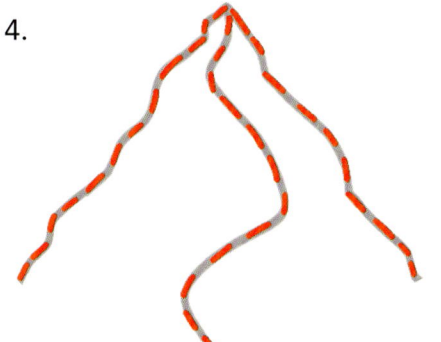

5.

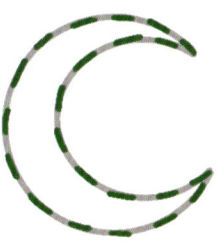

6.

Dragon Wings

Mask

Color Guide

Dark Purple
#29

Light Purple
#28

Pink
#3778

Green
#320

Mask

Stitch Guide

Steps

1.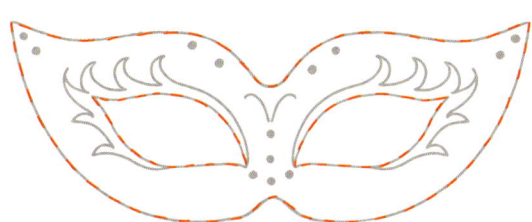

2.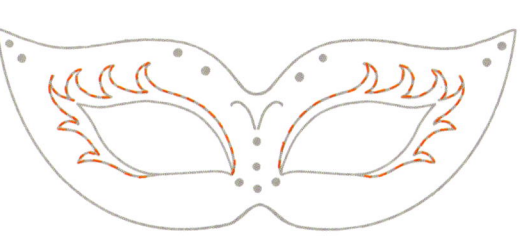

3.

4.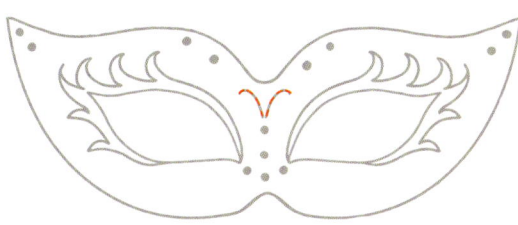

5.

6.

7.

8.

1. Split Stitch, 3-ply, #29
2. Split Stitch, 2-ply, #28
3. French Knot Stitch, 3-ply, #28
4. Split Stitch, 2-ply, #29
5. Satin Stitch, 2-ply, #3778
6. Split Stitch, 2-ply, #28
7. Satin Stitch, 2-ply, #28
8. Satin Stitch, 2-ply, #320

Mask 83

Skull and Books

Color Guide

Gold
#436

Red
#918

Light Blue
#926

Dark Blue
#930

Green
#3364

Black
#310

Skull and Books

Steps

1.

2. 　　3. 　　4. 　　5.

6. 　　7. 　　8.

9. 　10. 　11. 　12. 　13.

1. Split Stitch, 2-ply, #310
2. Split Stitch, 2-ply, #310
3. Split Stitch, 3-ply, #3364
4. Satin Stitch, 2-ply, #3364
5. Satin Stitch, 2-ply, #918
6. Satin Stitch, 2-ply, #436
7. Split Stitch, 2-ply, #BLANC
8. French Knot Stitch, 2-ply, #918
9. Satin Stitch, 2-ply, #926
10. Satin Stitch/Long Stitch, 2-ply, #930
11. Split Stitch, 1-ply, #310
12. Long Stitch, 2-ply, #926
13. Long Stitch, 1-ply, #310

Skull and Books

Sword and Wings

Color Guide

Black #310

Purple #154

Sword and Wings

Stitch Guide

Steps

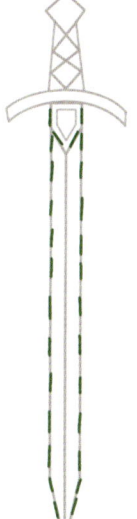
1.

2.

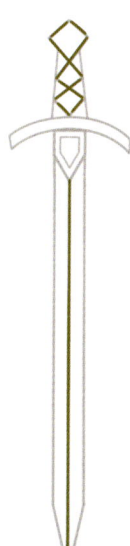
3.

1. Split Stitch, 2-ply, #310
2. Split Stitch, 2-ply, #310
3. Long Stitch, 1-ply, #310
4. Split Stitch, 2-ply, #154
5. Fill Stitch, 2-ply, #154
6. Split Stitch, 2-ply, #310
7. Split Stitch, 1-ply, #310

4.
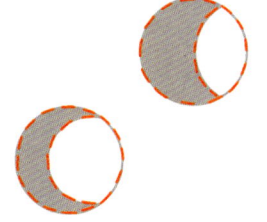

5.

6.

7.

Sword and Wings

Dragon Sword

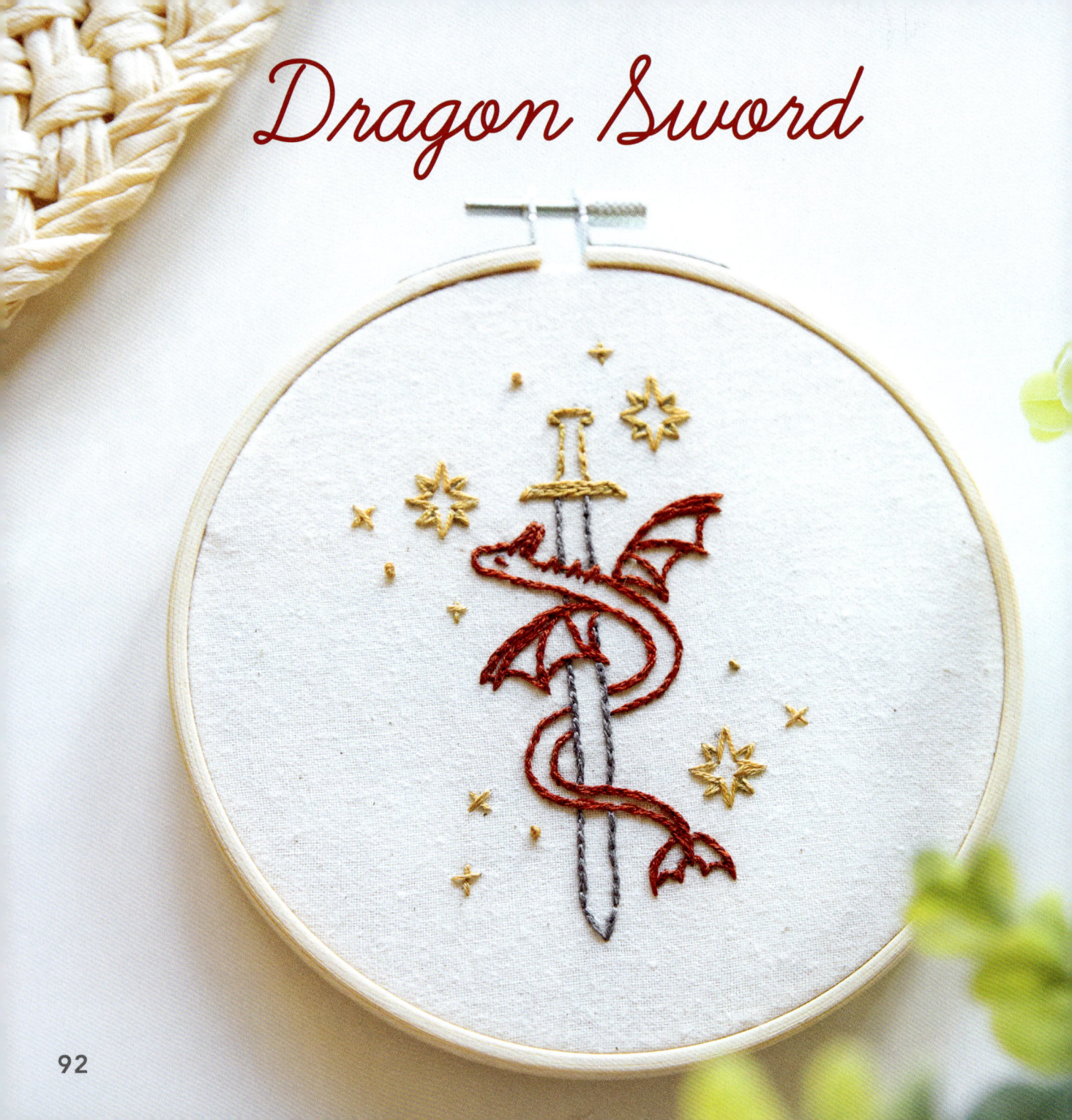

Color Guide

Red
#918

Gold
#729

Silver
#3011

Dragon Sword

Stitch Guide

Dragon Sword

Steps

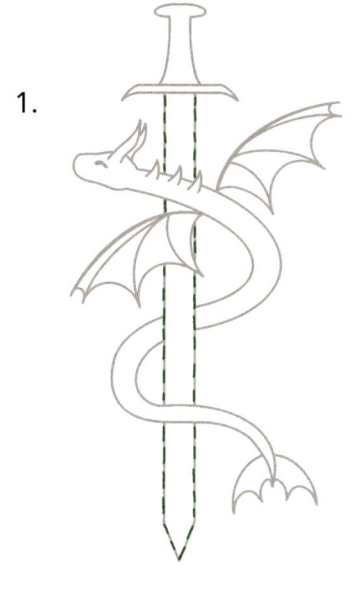

1. Split Stitch, 3-ply, #3011
2. Split Stitch, 3-ply, #729
3. Split Stitch, 2-ply, #918
4. Long Stitch, 3-ply, #729
5. Back Stitch, 2-ply, #729
6. French Knot Stitch, 3-ply, #729

Dragon Sword

Considerable Length

Color Guide

"*considerable length*"

Black
#310

Stitch Guide

Steps

1. Split Stitch, 1-ply, #310
2. French Knot Stitch, 1-ply, #310
3. Split Stitch, 2-ply, #310
4. Split Stitch, 1-ply, #310
5. Long Stitch, 2-ply, #310

1. "*considerable*

2. "*considerable*

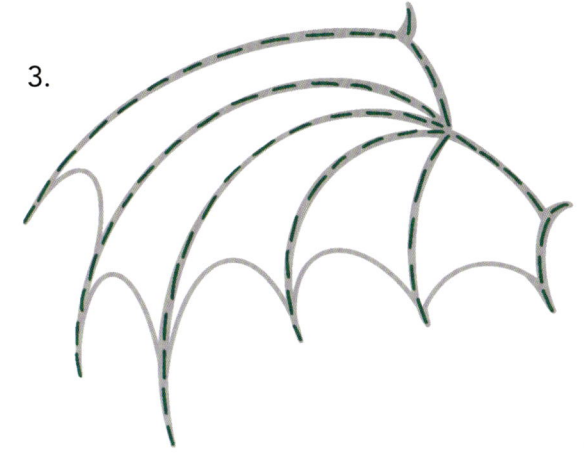

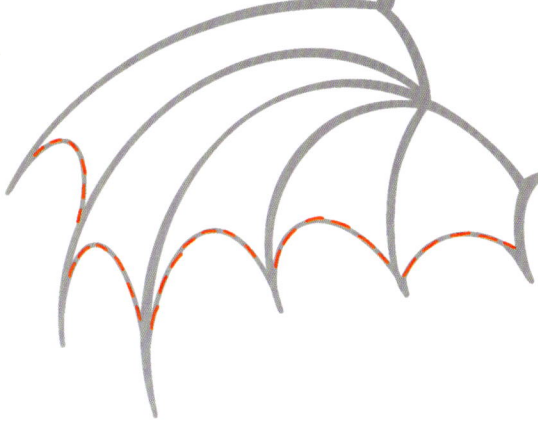

Considerable Length

Pine Cone

Color Guide

Grey
#648

Dark Brown
#839

Dark Green
#3011

Light Green
#3012

Light Brown
#3863

Pine Cone

Stitch Guide

Steps

1. Split Stitch, #648, 2-ply
2. Satin Stitch, #648, 2-ply
3. Split Stitch, #839, 2-ply
4. Split Stitch, #839, 1-ply
5. French Knot Stitch, #648, 2-ply
6. Split Stitch, 3863, 2-ply
7. Satin Stitch, #3011 + #3012, 2-ply

1.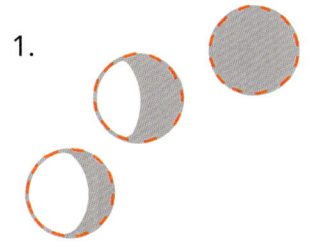

2.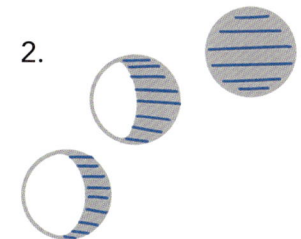

3.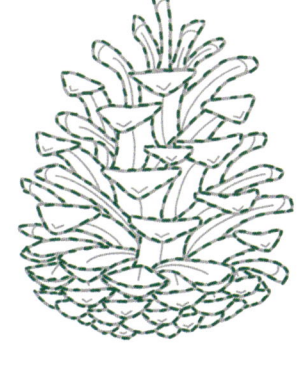

4.

5.

6.

7.

Templates

Teacup p. 12

Cauldron p. 16

Mountain Flower p. 20

Dragon Book p. 24

Darling p. 28

Heart Book p. 32

Painting p. 36

Through Love p. 40

Mushroom p. 44

Dragon Moon p. 48

Lily of the Valley   p. 52

Mage Hand p. 56

Lupine p. 60

Morally Grey p. 64

Angel Wings p. 72

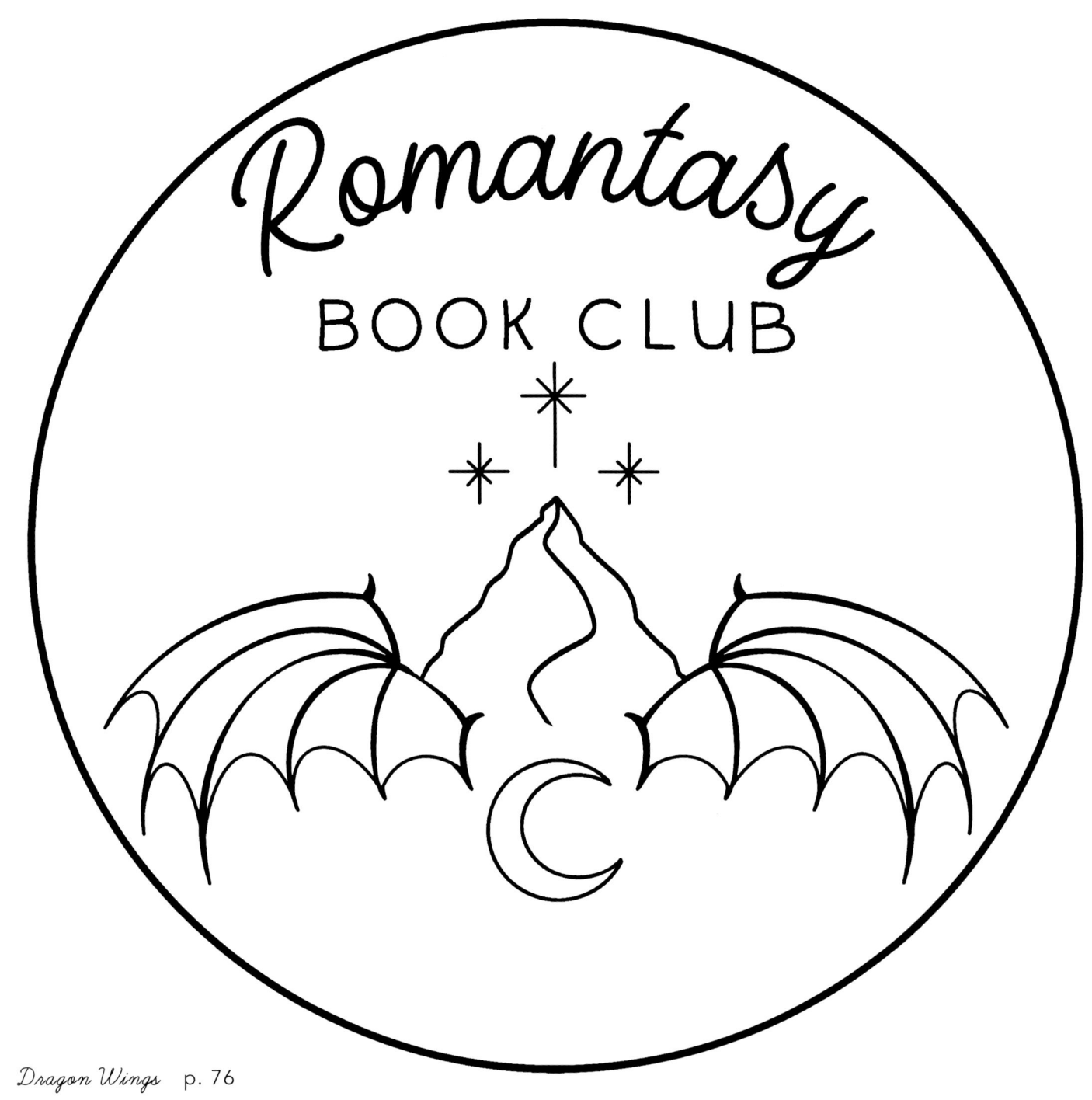

Dragon Wings p. 76

Mask   p. 80

Skull and Books p. 84

Sword and Wings   p. 88

Dragon Sword p. 92

Pine Cone p. 100